First published 1998 by Walker Books Ltd
87 Vauxhall Walk, London SE11 5HJ

2 4 6 8 10 9 7 5 3 1

This book has been typeset in Granjon.

Printed in Belgium

British Library Cataloguing in Publication Data
A catalogue record for this book is available
from the British Library.

ISBN 0-7445-5573-6

WALKER BOOKS
AND SUBSIDIARIES
LONDON • BOSTON • SYDNEY

ALLAN AHLBERG

MONKEY DO!

ILLUSTRATED BY

ANDRÉ AMSTUTZ

Sunny morning, bright and early,
Things are stirring in the zoo.

Comes the keeper with his key-ring,
Monkey see, Monkey do!

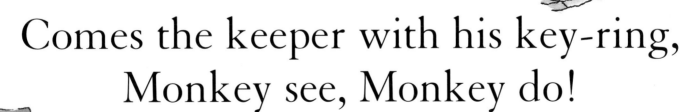

Here's a python,
here's a panda,
Here's a bouncy
kangaroo
With a pocket
full of mischief...

Monkey see, Monkey do!

Miss Giraffe
has had her breakfast,
Miss Giraffe
admires the view,
She just stands there
like a ladder,
Monkey see,
Monkey do!

Through the trees,
Up the street,
Busy fingers,
Busy feet.
Helping Harry,
Helping Sam,
Lady screaming –
Monkey scram!

Baby Biggins in his high chair
With his bib of baby blue

And a *beautiful banana* –
Monkey see, Monkey chew!

Mrs Biggins in a hurry,
Mrs Biggins in a stew,

Piles the kids into the Volvo,
Bags and pushchair –

Monkey too!

Down the street,
Up the road,
Noisy traffic,
Noisy load.

Crowded playground,
Kids galore,
Game of football –
Monkey score!

Mrs Murphy
in the morning,
Teaching tables,
two times two,

Puts the sums
up on the blackboard,
Monkey see,
Monkey do!

Monkey business in the morning,
Monkey business all day through.

Teachers worn out in the staffroom,
Tea and biscuits, Monkey too!

Tabby kitten up
a flagpole.

Crowd below all
going, "Oooh!"

Fireman trying hard
to reach him.

Monkey see,
Monkey do!

Getting late,
Sun is low,
Bye, bye kitten,
Time to go.

Up the road,
Down the lane,
Through the trees,
Home again.

Here's a zebra
with a carrot.

Here's a brown bear
with a bun.

Here's a crocodile with … nothing.
Monkey see…

Monkey

run!

Silver moon and starry evening,
Nothing stirring in the zoo.

Just one worn out little Monkey,
Wants his mummy, wouldn't you?

The End